BERTHA
and the
RACING PIGEON

For Stella and Tanya

Also by Pam Ayres

Some of Me Poetry
Some More of Me Poetry
Thoughts of a Late-Night Knitter
All Pam's Poems
(an omnibus comprising
Some of Me Poetry,
Some More of Me Poetry and
Thoughts of a Late-Night Knitter)

Hutchinson Junior Books Ltd
3 Fitzroy Square, London W1P 6JD

An imprint of the Hutchinson Publishing Group

London Melbourne Sydney Auckland
Wellington Johannesburg and agencies
throughout the world

First published 1979

Copyright © Pam Ayres 1979

Printed in Italy by A. Mondadori Editore, Verona

ISBN 0 09 139220 9

PAM AYRES

BERTHA
and the
RACING PIGEON

Hutchinson of London

1

Bertha sat outside the Barn one Spring morning, looking this way and that. This way were the chimneys and rooftops of Wanford town, and that way were the fields and green woods of Oxfordshire. Immediately underneath her was the Barn and Bertha lived in the Upper Right-Hand Corner. Sharing it was an Owl, Tired Melvin, who lived in the Lower Left-Hand Corner and Didn't Have Much to Say. Bertha was a Wood Pigeon. Not a Great Brain, you might say, but an honest, hardworking person, rather plain and kind. The sun was shining. It warmed the creamy stone tiles of the roof and lingered on the soft feathers round Bertha's neck, changing them from beautiful pink to beautiful green and back again.

Rapidly nearing Bertha from the north was a black dot with a marble clenched in its feet. Bertha watched it approach with some trepidation, recognizing the great spare frame of Soothsayer Rook. He could see into the future and would tell your fortune for you if you wanted, and also if you didn't want. Bertha's feathers blew about as he flapped up beside her, fighting to retain his marble and his balance. His own baggy trouser-leg feathers were ruffled by the struggle and stuck out askew.

'Good Grief,' he panted, great chalky beak agape, 'I've flown all the way from Over Yonder!'

'How lovely to see you ... ' began Bertha politely.

'No! No! ... don't speak!' cried Soothsayer Rook with much drama, eye to eye with the glass marble, 'the crystal ball is clearin'!'

Bertha peered over his shoulder at the chipped surface of the marble.

'Oh, Bertha,' he murmured, 'I can see Trouble in Store, I can see STRIFE, I can see a great CLOUD on the crystal ball. . . .'

'Perhaps you dropped it in something,' Bertha ventured.

'No, not that sort of cloud,' said Rook rather sharply. 'This cloud is almost upon you, Bertha! You must make preparations! I see a long journey ahead of you!' (Rook was warming to his subject now.) 'I see you flying far, far away, over the trees and great cities! I see a WORD, Bertha, it begins with P!'

'Puffed out?' she suggested helpfully.

Soothsayer Rook did not reply, but looked balefully up from the marble.

'The crystal ball never lies,' he said, eyes glinting at the other end of the beak. 'There is Them That Mock and then again there is Them That Believe. Time Will Tell,' and because Rook also saw himself as something of a poet he added ominously:

'Not so clever it do be,
To laugh at what in the crystal ball, I do see.'

He looked sternly at Bertha for a moment, then gripping the marble manfully between his feet he prepared to fly off.

'Can't you stay for a little while, Rook?' asked Bertha, who did *like* Rook even though at times she found him a little Difficult to Fathom. 'You could share a crust with me.'

'Thank you, no,' Rook replied, 'I'm off to see Sid Magpie. I always tell his fortune of a Tuesday you see, he depends on it. He won't get out of bed if I haven't been, for fear of doing the wrong thing. Goodbye!' he shouted as he flapped away to the wood.

'Funny old Rook,' thought Bertha watching him disappear. But there was something Bertha did not know. Everything Rook had predicted was going to come true.

2

Bertha went back into the barn. Down in the Lower Left-Hand Corner, Tired Melvin, looking very tired, was asleep. On hearing Bertha fly up to her corner, he woke up.

'Is it the hours of darkness?' he asked.

'No, not yet,' replied Bertha kindly, 'it's only the morning.'

He re-arranged his feathers and went back to sleep. Bertha studied him across the barn. Melvin's life was all a mite unhealthy, she decided. He slept right through the bright day, only emerging when it was twilight or dark. And when he returned to the barn in the early morning, if you looked closely you could see dried blood on his beak and in the feathers of his feet.

By now Bertha was hungry so she flew over the fields to Wanford. There, she would potter round the Market Place picking up bits. On a good day people threw crumbs. On a bad day she would meet the two evil brothers, Andy and Quickbuck Harris, who threw stones and horrid fag-ends. But on an extra specially fine and wonderful day she would meet the road sweeper, Jack Broom. He was a big kind man in a black jacket and cap, who never went around hurting things. Jack pushed his truck full of brooms and spades, swept the town and kept it looking ship-shape.

Most lunchtimes, if he was out that way, he was to be found sitting under the statue of King Alfred in the Market Place, and he would keep an eye open for Bertha. Jack Broom had a good wife and a small appetite, which usually meant he had sandwiches left over from his lunch. These great wonderful doorsteps he would break up and feed to Bertha, and he would talk to her in a low voice if nobody was about. Considering that one was a man and one was a pigeon, it was all very close and friendly.

Today, flying into town, Bertha was delighted to see him in his usual place and she flew down to his feet.

'Well ... hullo!' said Jack Broom, feeling in his dinner-bag for a sandwich. 'Are you on your own *again*? It's about time you found yourself a *mate*, now it's Spring and all.' And it was true. Bertha didn't have a mate. Sometimes it could grow very lonely in the Upper Right-Hand Corner.

3

That afternoon she was sitting on the Barn digesting Jack Broom's sandwich in the sunshine and wondering whether to fly over to The Gravel Pit for a bath. Scanning the blue sky idly she noticed another black dot approaching from the north.

'Soothsayer Rook again?' she wondered. 'But I've had my fortune told once today.'

But it wasn't Soothsayer Rook, it wasn't big enough. Furthermore, it wasn't flying a very straight course. In fact, whoever it was didn't appear to be flying very well at all, but was tumbling about in a most extraordinary fashion.

As it came closer Bertha could see it was a pigeon. Not an

ordinary pigeon like herself, but a larger bird, a different colour and more fancy altogether.

The poor bird struggled nearer, heading for the Barn. Bertha hoped it hadn't been shot. Shot birds were very distressing because there wasn't much you could do, as a pigeon.

At the entrance to the Barn the stranger faltered and seemed to give up altogether, fluttering down to the earth and lying very still. He was a brown and white racing pigeon with a ring round one leg. Bertha stared worriedly as he miserably puffed up his feathers and closed his eyes. Then she flew down and, keeping a little distance away because after all you never *knew*, walked round him looking for shot wounds. Luckily she could see none. Edging a little closer she asked in a small voice, 'Can I help you at all?'

The brown and white pigeon opened an eye.

'Is this the Loft?' he said.

'No,' replied Bertha rather uncertainly, not knowing what a Loft was, 'it's the Barn.'

'Oh,' he said in a small disappointed voice. 'I'm lost then.'

'Where are you going?' asked Bertha.

'Birmingham. I'm in a race.'

'Whatever happened?' Bertha wanted to know.

'There was a storm at the start, a really bad one. We were all blown about but I lost a flight feather. When the storm cleared my companions were gone. I couldn't keep up you see, I couldn't fly a proper straight course.'

Bertha inspected the beautiful brown and white speckled wing. Sure enough there was a great gap instead of the important flight feather pigeons steer with.

'Do you happen,' asked the racing pigeon, 'to have any food to spare at all?'

'Oh yes!' declared Bertha, delighted to be able to help, and flying to the Upper Right-Hand Corner she collected a Jack Broom crust she'd been saving for a rainy day. When she dropped it in front of him they found he was too weak to pull it apart on his own so Bertha kindly stood on one end.

She was uneasy about them being on the ground though, for it was full of danger, frequented by dogs, foxes and men. So when he had eaten all of the giant crust she urged him to fly up into the barn out of harm's way. 'You can rest there and be safe,' she said encouragingly. So with a great last effort the brown and white pigeon flew lopsidedly to the shade of the Upper Right-Hand Corner. His poor body was thin and light. Bertha settled close by him to stop him from falling off.

'I'll look after you,' she said. 'My name's Bertha. I live here.'

'You are very kind,' he replied. 'My name is Fleet. I'm a racing pigeon from Birmingham. Actually,' he added, 'I'm a Red-Checkered Racing Homer.'

Bertha searched desperately for the right thing to say.

'Good Gracious!' she said in the end. But Fleet was asleep so it didn't matter.

Their conversation had disturbed Tired Melvin, however, who woke up crossly. 'Some people,' he announced sternly across the barn, 'have no consideration for birds of Nocturnal Habits!'

'For *what?*' asked Bertha, baffled.

'For Birds That Fly by Night,' he snapped. 'For the Night Shift!'

So Bertha stayed awake in the barn whilst Tired Melvin and Fleet, the racing pigeon, slept on.

4

It was far into the morning when Fleet woke up. He looked a great deal better. Bertha gave him another crust and said, 'Don't feel you have to Rush Off, Fleet. You are most welcome to stay at the Barn until you've rested and your wing feather has grown.' Besides, she liked him. He was a lovely big bird with brown and white speckles like lace over his wings. He was polite and handsome and Bertha thought he was wonderful. He didn't seem to know very much about living in a barn, however.

'When do they feed us?' he asked.

'Who?' said Bertha.

'Well, whoever feeds you here.'

'Nobody feeds me, Fleet,' she replied. 'I sort of feed myself. Why, does somebody feed you?'

'Why yes,' he answered, surprised. 'They come to feed us at six o'clock in the Loft. They give us beans and peas and maize.'

'Oh,' said Bertha, trying to picture this loft without much success. 'What do you have to do as a racing pigeon then?'

'You have to fly about,' Fleet replied matter-of-factly.

'Fly about?'

'Yes, the man puts us in boxes on a lorry or a train and we are taken a long way from home, oh hundreds of miles sometimes, then they let us all out together and we have to fly home again.'

Bertha thought about it.

'Why?' she asked.

'Why what?'

'Why do you have to do that?'

'Because the man wants us to. That's why he gives us the beans and peas and maize. We keep flying home and he keeps looking after us. That's what a racing pigeon's life is like.'

'What happens to you if you don't get home on time?' Bertha asked, feeling rather uneasy.

Fleet held his head up. 'Oh, you have to go away for Retraining and Rehabilitation,' he said airily. 'They come and get you in a Special Bag. All the old pigeons and the ones who lose their way have to go and be retrained. Only I think afterwards you go on somewhere else. You don't come back to the Loft anyway. It's funny really,' Fleet said quietly, 'the way nobody ever comes back, not even for five minutes, to say hello.'

For some reason Bertha hated the sound of the Loft and the Special Bag, and looking across at Fleet she caught a strange frightened look in his eye, too.

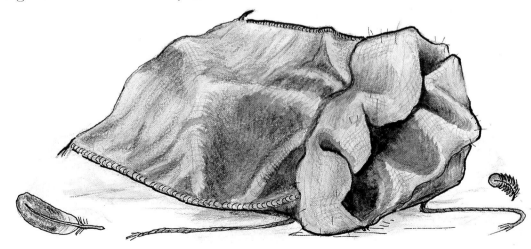

5

So Bertha and Fleet became friends and stayed together at the barn. They sat side by side in the sunshine and flew into Wanford, very slowly because of Fleet's missing feather, to feed in the Market Place.

Jack Broom the road sweeper was very pleased to meet Fleet.

'So you found yourself a mate then?' he teased Bertha, 'and a fine handsome fellow too. He needs fattening up a bit though!'

So Jack brought more sandwiches still to the statue of King Alfred, which pleased Mrs Broom who thought Jack must be eating sensibly at last.

One day when Jack was feeding his pigeons, he was sorry to see the two rotten brothers, Andy and Quickbuck Harris, strolling towards him. Jack didn't like them at all, didn't like the look of them, didn't like the way they lounged round the town all day doing nothing. Quickbuck Harris was a big stout man with a shock of dark curly hair and an ugly, lopsided grin. Andy Harris was bald with white eyebrows. He was passionately interested in cowboys and at night in his narrow, sagging bed he would clutch the thin grey sheet and imagine himself astride a great stallion. In his dreams he rode the range wearing chaps and a sardonic smile. In actual fact he

was very weak and did as his brother told him. But because of his consuming love for anything to do with the Wild West, Andy Harris permanently wore cowboy boots and a pair of giant tin spurs, which the cheapjack on the Saturday Market assured him had been sent straight from Texas, direct.

As they sat down either side of Jack, Bertha nudged Fleet nervously. 'Come away, Fleet,' she said quickly and made him leave the crusts on the ground and fly off. 'They mean us no good,' she told him, 'I can feel it. Be very careful of them.'

'Still chasing the birds then, Jack?' asked Quickbuck grinning. Jack didn't answer, but chewed silently on his sandwiches.

'That brown and white one looked like a racing pigeon,' said Quickbuck slyly. 'Good bird, that. Expensive.'

'Is it?' said Jack non-committally, and standing up he walked over to his truck and pushed it away.

Behind him, under the statue of King Alfred, the Harris brothers remained, Quickbuck deep in thought, Andy shallow.

'What do you say, my son,' asked Quickbuck fondly of his brother, 'to a pint of bitter ale, with a fine head perhaps just overflowing at the top of the glass?'

Andy sat bolt upright, a radiant smile transforming his face. 'Ooooh yes!' he cried jubilantly.

'Right!' decided Quickbuck, slapping Andy on the back and springing to his feet. 'It's your round. I forgot me wallet!'

Quickbuck's hysterical laughter could be heard all the way to the pub.

6

The Harris brothers' local was a pub called the Rod and Maggot. It was owned by a very stout man called Circumference Smith, known to his friends as Smiffy. Smiffy had an Afghan Hound because he admired its grace and lissom beauty. It was called Sheik Wish Ida Bought One and it dug holes. This greatly irritated Smiffy who had expected the Sheik to stand about looking posh. The Sheik had no time for such fruitless pastimes. Day and night he laboured, digging holes, great clods of mud clanging about his person as he worked. The deeper the hole grew, the more useful and saintly the Sheik felt.

Smiffy had long since stopped filling them in. Now the back yard of the pub was pitted with craters like a bomb site, and the Sheik dug on. He was working on a fine hole now, a hole to set the heart singing with joy. He tore feverishly at the turf with his teeth, shaking the soil this way and that, front feet working like pistons and his long cream coat congealed into a giant muddy slab on his back. He did not even notice as the Harris brothers stumbled past on their way home singing the haunting refrain, 'Unfurl the Banner Son, your Mother's Joined Up.' But he did look up guiltily as Smiffy approached, hands on hips. A beaten man, Smiffy hooked a stick through the Sheik's mud-thickened collar and led him away to be

hosed down. Behind them, water seeped into the bottom of the hole.

Some time later the Sheik, clean and beautiful, and with the loving thrum of the hosepipe ringing in his ears, swept past the blocked drain in the yard, to pause at the pub gate. He looked up at the church clock which, having no hands, was simple for a dog to understand. Just time for a walk before the afternoon's dig! He tossed his elegant blond mane and trotted off alone to his own private place of worship, the biggest hole for miles around, the deepest! the most wonderful! Oxfordshire's answer to the Grand Canyon ... Wanford Gravel Pit! With a flourish of his silken tail he was gone.

7

Bertha didn't want to think about Fleet going back to Birmingham. She liked him very much. Life was altogether nicer with a friend, and at night they sat on the beam in the Upper Right-Hand Corner and slept close together for comfort and warmth.

They didn't talk about Birmingham at all. Yet Fleet had been living at the Barn for some days now, he was fully recovered and he could fly. Clearly sooner or later they would have to discuss What Was to Become of Fleet. For now though it had all been brushed under the carpet.

Today it was very hot and they flew south to Wanford Gravel Pit for a bath. One end of the Pit had been turned into a rubbish dump and was full of wailing seagulls from Foreign Parts, but at the other end the water was shallow and clean. There was a yellow gravel beach under the cliff where the pigeons could take a bath and dry off in the sunshine. It was a perfect spot. Bertha and Fleet stayed for much of the summer afternoon, fluffing their feathers and splashing in the water.

Only once was the peace disturbed when a seagull strayed near them and screamed 'No Fish!' in a funny accent, but then they were funny birds altogether.

Then Fleet said, 'Time to go home,' and Bertha looked up frightened in case he meant Birmingham.

'Oh, Fleet!' she blurted, 'oh, Fleet, don't go home! It would be so lonely in the Barn. I didn't mind before because I'd never *had* a friend but I should miss you so much now, there'd be no one to talk to or do things with. Well, I mean, there'd be Melvin of course, but he's an Owl and Rather Difficult. Besides,' Bertha went on, ' the Loft doesn't sound right to me, the way they take the old birds away in a Special Bag and they don't ever come back. Oh don't go, Fleet,' Bertha said fearfully, 'stay in the Barn and don't go back.'

'I wasn't going to go back, Bertha,' Fleet said quietly. 'I don't want to race any more. If you didn't want me I was going to go to Trafalgar Square. But I like it here, it's green and fresh and nice. Birmingham is all lorries and smoke and roads. And I'd miss you too, you're the best friend I've ever had.'

And so, on the yellow beach at Wanford Gravel Pit, they decided that Fleet would be a Racing Pigeon (Retired) and that he and Bertha would Pair Up, build a nest in the Barn and lay eggs which was altogether the proper thing for pigeons to do. Bertha was so overcome with relief that she walked off and had another bath to help her collect herself.

Fleet, like many other racing pigeons, had the name and telephone number of his Loft stamped on his wing in black ink. They sensed this was not a good thing. 'Let me have a proper look at it,' said Bertha. Fleet spread out his beautiful speckled wing with the ugly square of writing which read:

PERCY GRIMCAT, PIGEON FANCIER OF NOTE
PLEASE RING 021-331-9730

'Let's see if it washes off,' suggested Bertha, nudging Fleet out into the water. But though they preened and wetted it in the Gravel Pit the writing remained as black and clear as ever.

'It's no good,' Bertha admitted, coughing up a feather, 'it doesn't wash off. Perhaps it will wear off, Fleet.'

Another problem of course was the ring round his leg which identified him as the property of Percy Grimcat. No end of tugging could get if off. It was too late. The rings were put on when the pigeons were babies with small flexible feet and Fleet was fully grown now. So the ring, too, had to stay. 'Never mind,' Bertha said as they prepared to fly back to the Barn, 'I don't expect Percy Grimcat will come looking for you here.'

Suddenly both pigeons froze as the grasses along the top of the cliff parted to reveal, not the face of Percy Grimcat, but the long body of Sheik Wish Ida Bought One, gliding along the cliff edge, head held high. Always a dog with a fertile imagination, the Sheik was in a world of his own. He surveyed the vast Gravel Pit; it stretched as far as the Afghan eye could see. The

Sheik was dreaming that he himself had dug it all and that *this* was his long-awaited triumphant appearance before the adoring crowds. Their cheers resounded all about him! As he swept along, nose forced high in the sky, why, he could hear them gasp and whisper, 'Look! Is that the dog who dug Wanford Gravel Pit? . . . . Was it *this* wonderful dog?'

The applause and admiration of the imaginary crowd was *deafening* in his ears as the sandy cliff edge gave way beneath his feet and he plunged into the Gravel Pit. It was a rude awakening. He landed in a great yelping ball of legs and ears on the little beach beside Bertha and Fleet. They flew back in alarm. The Sheik's head appeared from the ball, stunned, blinking.

'Are you a Hastronomer?' asked Bertha warily.

'A what?' snapped the Sheik.

'We thought you must be studying the stars,' explained Fleet, and when the Sheik didn't reply he added, 'You seemed to be looking up at the sky.'

'Something caught my attention,' announced the Sheik grandly, trying to cover the fact that he felt rather foolish. 'But no, the stars hold no fascination for me – I am an Excavationist!'

'Oh,' nodded the pigeons, interested.

'An excavationist, eh?' remarked Bertha.

'Oh yes,' declared the Sheik darkly, walking towards the Pit Entrance Gate limping in four legs and an ear. 'Make no mistake ... I am the Dog for the Job!'

They watched him disappear. 'What an odd dog,' Bertha said. 'What's an excavationist, Fleet?'

Fleet said after only a moment's hesitation, 'Oh, it means you used to be a cavationist but you're not now.'

And together they flew home to the barn.

8

One day they had a visitor. It was Soothsayer Rook, in a dreadful state.

'I've lost me crystal ball!' he gasped, looking distractedly this way and that. 'It dropped out of me feet in the rain!'

'Oh dear, I am sorry,' exclaimed Bertha. 'Where did you lose it?'

'Over by the Fruit Pie Factory,' gabbled Soothsayer. 'Oh, whatever shall I *do*? I don't know what's going to happen from one day to the next. It's a fearful business, it's me livelihood gone! All my customers they come to me and ask, 'What shall I do about this or that Soothsayer?' and I can't advise them! I'm losing all CREDIBILITY! Oh, Cor blimey! Oh, strike a light!' Soothsayer grew more frantic as he spoke, dancing sideways and then back, folding his wings and then waving them about.

'Well,' suggested Bertha, 'perhaps you could see into the future with something else.'

'There's only the tea leaves,' said Rook hopelessly, 'and what about the problem of transportation? I mean it's one thing carrying the crystal ball, I can manage that all right, but it's another thing entirely to carry a bundle of tea leaves! I

drop them! Me feet are too big! When I get to where I'm going, I haven't any left!'

'Oh, I am sorry,' said Bertha, 'we'll be sure to keep a look out whenever we're near the Fruit Pie Factory.'

'Yes, we will,' added Fleet, 'we'll look out for it all the time.'

'Oh, you're good friends to me,' Soothsayer Rook declared, 'and I shan't forget it.' Raising his head solemnly, he recited:

'They'll seek my crystal ball for me
Here, there, everywhere, but specially at the Fruit Pie Factory.'

He recited the second line very fast so as to make it fit.

'Goodbye,' said Bertha and Fleet, a little taken aback, and watched poor Rook flap off to see Sid Magpie who had a sharp eye for anything bright and might be able to spot it too.

9

Bertha was by now expecting eggs, and growing rather stout. The pigeons built a strong nest of twigs up in the corner and Bertha sat in it to wait. One day after much effort, she laid them. There were two, very round and white and altogether something to be proud of. They had to be sat upon with great care all the time, to keep them warm and safe, and to ensure they would hatch out into fine babies.

Bertha and Fleet took it in turns, one sitting on the eggs while the other flew out to feed. By the end of the second week, the eggs began to rumble mysteriously and move, ever so slightly, in the nest.

Even Tired Melvin took an interest.

'You've got eggs, I see, you and that mate of yours.'

'Yes,' replied Bertha rather proudly, 'we're expecting them to hatch out any day now.'

'Yes, well I realize that These Things Happen,' said Melvin importantly, 'but I do *hope* that these offspring of yours are not going to Kick up a Racket during Unsociable Hours.'

'Pardon?' said Bertha, troubled as usual by the Owl's turn of phrase.

'I hope they don't wake me up!' he snapped, 'for I am a bird that sleeps by day and Walks by Night.'

'Oh no,' she agreed, 'I won't let them do that.'

'What time is it?' asked Melvin.

'About afternoon,' replied Bertha.

10

Meanwhile, back at the Rod and Maggot, Sheik Wish Ida Bought One was aglow with joy and fulfilment as he surveyed the hole he had dug. Never in all his career had he dug for so long without hitting rock or Fools' Gold. He sat on the edge, indistinguishable from the heaped mud on all sides. Why, it was more than a hole, it was a Pit, a Chasm, a feat of engineering unrivalled in the history of dog. A muddy slurry lapped in the bottom. It was finished. An expression of supreme peace transformed his mud-encrusted face as Sheik Wish Ida Bought One, Artist, stepped delicately away to wait by the hose pipe.

11

On the fifteenth day after Bertha laid the eggs, it dawned very blowy and there was hard rain in the wind. As the day progressed, a gale blew up, and the wind wailed round the barn tearing at a loose sheet of metal on one side so that it clanged and banged in a sudden, startling fashion. The barn was wet and running with rain.

These were hard days for the pigeons. No longer could they spend easy afternoons at the nice end of the Gravel Pit, nor could they linger in the sunshine on the barn roof. The eggs couldn't be left, not for a minute. Once they grew cold the babies inside would die and the eggs would turn sour and useless in the nest. So they continued into the third week, the long still hours sitting in the Upper Right-Hand Corner, and the hurried flights out to snatch what food they could find. The pigeons grew thin and light.

In the late afternoon, Bertha, battling with the wind and cold rain, struggled back to take over from Fleet. She flew in gratefully from the wildness outside to the warm peace of the barn.

'Oh, Fleet, be careful,' she said. 'It's a dreadful day and this wind blows us like paper now we are so thin.'

'I'll take care,' he said, 'but I am so hungry, I must go. I'll try to find Jack Broom in the town.'

And Fleet flew out of the barn into the storm, leaving Bertha in the dim corner, uneasy.

Outside the wind wrenched the loose metal this way and that, rattling and slamming it violently against the barn wall. Tired Melvin puffed up his feathers and turned his face closer in to the wall, trying to sleep. Bertha nudged the eggs around and then settled down to watch the door for Fleet's return.

Only Fleet wasn't coming back.

12

Down in the town a siren blew to tell the workers in the Allpastry and Gap Fruit Pie Factory that it was time to go home. The great double doors opened and men and women poured out all dressed in white overalls to keep the pies clean. They hurried along in the wind, their heads bent down against the rain.

One of the ladies from the factory had a little boy running beside her. The lady was very cold and anxious to get home. The little boy was equally anxious to go to the shop for some toffees. 'Can we go, Mum? Can I *have* some toffees, Mum?'

'No, you can't!' she said sharply. 'I'm not going to the shop in this weather, and anyway, toffees rot your teeth!'

'Oh, *Mum*!' cried the small boy and angrily kicked a tuffet of grass beside the path. After his mother had hurried him on impatiently, a large bright marble rolled out of the grass and lay clearly in the road.

13

It was there that Fleet saw it as he fought his way into the town. He knew straight away that it was Soothsayer Rook's crystal ball. For a moment, he couldn't decide what to do. He was very cold and hungry. He wanted to find food and return quickly to the Barn. On the other hand he remembered poor Rook dancing backwards and forwards, worried and unhappy as he told them of the loss. Fleet thought how overjoyed Rook would be to have it back. It wouldn't take long to return it to his house, high in the dead elms in the wood. Fleet swooped down, picked it up with some difficulty and turned towards the wood. He flew awkwardly against the dreadful wind. When he arrived at the great elm where Rook lived he was wet and more tired than ever.

But Rook couldn't believe it. He looked at the marble and looked again. A great tear of joy ran down his chalky old beak in the rain, and crying:

     'Glad, glad, I'm ever so glad

     To have back the crystal ball which before I lost it I had,'

he laid it tenderly and ever so carefully beside him in the branches. He thanked Fleet again and again for his trouble.

'I would give you all my stored-up food,' he said gratefully to Fleet, 'only I haven't got any.'

Fleet flew down from the elm and made for the town, weary and wet. The wind roared loudly about him as he came down into the Market Place.

Back up in the elm Soothsayer danced sideways along the branch in his baggy trousers, relieved and happy. After a little while he rushed fondly to the crystal ball to catch up on what was happening. He peered into it. The happiness melted away from his face. He wiped it with his wing to make sure that the rain wasn't affecting what he could see. But it wasn't. The awful picture was there in the crystal ball, as plain as day.

'Fleet!' cried Soothsayer. 'Fleet . . . come back!' The wind moaned round the black dead branches of his home. Soothsayer Rook was too late. Andy and Quickbuck Harris had already spotted Fleet feeding hungrily in the Market Place.

14

Fleet never heard them coming because of the wind, and he never saw them because he was so busy picking up food. He was totally engrossed in what he was doing when two great oily hands closed round him and snatched him up from the ground. Fleet stared, terrified, into the dreadful face of Quick-buck Harris.

'Well, now,' he grinned, 'what have we got here? A little *racing* pigeon if I'm not much mistaken.' Fleet could hardly breathe from fright and the man's tight grasp. Andy Harris roughly prised Fleet's wing from Quickbuck's hands and spread it out. The square of printed information showed up clear and black, and the brothers craned their necks to read it.

'All the way from Birmingham,' confirmed Quickbuck, 'stamped with a telephone number and all.' He smiled, and leaning over took a tenpenny piece from his brother's pocket. 'I think, Andy my son, that we might make a telephone call in the direction of Birmingham.' He stuffed Fleet down into his dark musty pocket and they sauntered off towards the phone box on the other side of the square.

In doing so they passed Jack Broom pushing his truck home, fed up with the rain.

'I *see*, Mr Grimcat,' Quickbuck was saying into the telephone in his best voice. 'A prize bird of yours, is it? And you'd like me to send him back to you? Well, now,' and he winked across the kiosk to his brother, 'you must realize that for a busy, hardworking person such as myself, Time is Money, and that perhaps some small encouragement. . . .' He gulped as Mr Grimcat spoke, then quickly recovered himself. '*Twenty pounds*? Why, yes, indeed, twenty pounds should just about cover the cost of my trouble. And you'll put the money in the post as soon as the pigeon arrives? Harris House, Wanford, Oxon, yes, that's right. Oh no, a bargain's a bargain sir. I shall put this pigeon on the next train. To where? Ah, you'd like him sent to Paddington. Right away, Mr Grimcat. A *pleasure* to do business with you. Goodbye.'

He replaced the phone and leered at Andy. 'Twenty pounds, my son,' he said. 'Come along, we've got a little parcel to wrap up. Twenty *pounds*! Whatever will you do with your five?' Patting his pocket happily, Quickbuck sauntered off home. Andy followed, adding up on his fingers in a puzzled fashion.

15

Bertha woke with a start as Soothsayer Rook clattered into the Barn.

'Oh, Bertha! Dreadful news!' he cried, dropping his crystal ball in the corner and rushing to the nest. 'They've got Fleet!'

Bertha came over cold. Outside, the tin rattled against the wall. 'Fleet?' she repeated. *'Who's* got him?'

'Andy and Quickbuck Harris, Bertha!' he gasped, running sideways up and down the beam. 'Oh, *do* something!'

'Do?' whispered Bertha, shocked. 'What can I do? The eggs. . . . Oh, Rook, are you *sure?*'

He nodded violently. 'He found my crystal ball, Bertha, and after he'd gone I could see he was in dreadful danger and I flew after him but I was too *late*, they'd got him and I hadn't warned him! The sparrows said he didn't even see them coming, it's awful!'

'But why would they *want* Fleet?' Bertha began and then stopped, realizing. 'Oh, *Rook*,' she said, 'he's got that address on his wing. They'll send him back!' They stared at each other blankly.

'I must go after him,' she decided. 'But my eggs, they're all ready to hatch, who will sit on them if I'm away?'

Just then there was a stirring from the Lower Left-Hand Corner. They both looked over as Tired Melvin woke up and demanded, 'What on *earth* is going on in this barn?' Bertha and Soothsayer exchanged one glance, then flew over to Melvin, settling one on each side of him.

Shortly afterwards, Bertha and Soothsayer Rook swooped down out of the Barn, with Rook peering through the rain at the crystal ball. 'Over there, the railway station,' he cawed against the noise of the wind.

Behind them, in the Upper Right-Hand Corner of the Barn, Tired Melvin was sprawled awkwardly over the two eggs, shouting crossly, 'What do you think I am? ... Mother Hen?'

16

Fleet was in a shoe box, tied up with string and marked FRAJILE. Quickbuck Harris had poked his finger through the lid to let some air come in, but had then wrapped the box in brown paper, so it didn't.

It was hot and horrible and Fleet was frightened. The box smelled of burning because all the time he was being wrapped up a great bonfire had smouldered in the garden of Harris House, and some of the smell had crept in.

The box was in a pile of other parcels on Platform 1 of Wanford Road Station, waiting for the 6.30 p.m. fast train to Paddington.

17

The stationmaster was called Archie Shadbolt. He had a very bad temper indeed. The men who worked at the station walked in fear of upsetting him because, once upset, a terrible change would sweep over Archie. His great fists would clench and unclench in an effort to keep away from the victim's neck, his big brown eyes would swell, glisten and roll backwards out of sight. Then he would throw back his head and shout. It was a fearful blast. Nobody could actually understand what Archie *said* when his shouting was at its finest, but it was easy to pick up the general idea if you were close by. Or equally, if you were not.

But this evening he was calm and serene as he sat in his office, drinking tea from a cracked mug and looking through his window down the windswept line for the 6.30 p.m. fast train to Paddington. For a moment his view was interrupted as the figure of Harry Crackitt, the porter, ran past the window. He always ran past it so that Archie would think he was rushed off his feet, but he forgot that Archie could hear him *walking* to the window in his great clumping boots before actually sprinting past it.

Archie Shadbolt was concerned about Harry and suspected he was a Secret Drinker. For hadn't Harry recently taken up playing the harp? The harp, mark you. And had he not one

day rashly brought the instrument in to the station to show his mates?

Archie cringed at the memory of Harry lurching down Platform 1 beneath the enormous harp. They could have passed it off as someone's luggage yet, but Harry had insisted on playing, astride it outside the Lost and Found Office, plucking and sighing as night fell. Furthermore it had proved a disturbingly eerie sight for passengers passing through the station. Several saw it as a portent, disembarking at the next stop.

'Was this,' Archie Shadbolt asked himself in the dusty office, 'was this the Right Way for a normal sober man to Go On? And more particularly, was it the Right Way for a man working at *his* railway station?' He growled into the cracked mug and his good humour vanished as the 6.30 pulled in at Platform 1.

18

Poor Fleet could not see the train as it pulled in and only heard the dreadful roaring and hissing. He waited inside the shoe box for something to happen.

Up came Harry Crackitt, whistling piercingly through his yellow rabbit teeth, and began to load the parcels into the freight compartment of the train. Fleet lurched wildly as the shoe box was snatched up. Because he was frightened and hungry, and because he could see nothing but the nightmare picture of Bertha waiting for him in the barn, he sat up as best he could, squawking and crying and flapping his wings in bitter protest. Though he did not realize it, this was really the cleverest thing he could have done, because sitting on the station roof scanning the heaps of parcels desperately were a thin lady pigeon and a rook with a marble. They heard the flapping coming from the box.

'There, look, Bertha! That parcel there!' cried Soothsayer, and they watched helplessly as Harry carried it into the wagon. Soothsayer made up his mind. 'Come on, Bertha,' he

PARCELS →

cried and in a flash they flew down, straight past the startled man's face, into the wagon and up on some mailbags at the back.

Harry stared at them in amazement. 'Shoo!' he shouted, waving his arm indignantly, but the birds stood fast, Bertha trembling a bit.

Harry was unnerved. 'SHOO!' he hollered again peering and blinking across the gloomy wagon. Bertha and Rook sat stoutly together on the mailbag. Harry gulped. He didn't like it at all. It wasn't natural! He slammed the door tightly shut and they heard his heavy footsteps running along the platform to fetch someone else. They were trapped. Bertha nudged closer to Rook, and they waited.

19

Seconds later Archie Shadbolt heard the clumping footsteps stop outside his office. Without so much as a knock the door was wrenched open, disregarding the Privacy of Rank, to reveal the white face of Harry Crackitt, springing agitatedly from side to side while his arms remained in the same place.

'Oh, Mr Shadbolt, Mr Shadbolt!' cried Harry.

Archie put his mug gently down on the table as his fists began to close solidly. He looked enquiringly up at the porter. 'Yes?' he replied with great control. Harry sensed what was coming and grew yet more flustered.

'Mr Shadbolt, sir! They won't come out! I just seen them and they won't come out! They just looks at you!'

'WHO?' roared the stationmaster.

'A pigeon and a rook with a marble in his feet! In the freight van!'

All Archie's worst fears were confirmed. The man *must* be drunk to talk such rubbish!

An earth-shattering bellow of rage echoed round the station and in the waiting room the fire came on. A mildewed photograph of the Chain Pier at Brighton fell to the floor in the Ladies as Harry Crackitt, pinned to the office wall by the blast, watched the great gorged jugulars on Archie's neck emerge round and perfect, and wondered if he would ever again hear the sweet note of the harp.

And against this stormy backdrop the 6.30 p.m. fast train to Paddington, firm and sealed, glided out of the station.

20

'He never came back,' Bertha breathed disbelievingly as the train gathered speed.

'What could have happened to him?' wondered Soothsayer from his mailbag. 'I thought he would be back in no time.'

Weak with relief, they gazed round the gloomy wagon as it clattered towards Paddington.

'Where are you, Fleet? called Bertha, and from a corner came a fluttering from the shoe-box-shaped parcel marked FRAJILE. Soothsayer perched on it and tore at the brown paper and string. Reaching the lid of the box, he put his great beak carefully into the air-hole and ripped out a big patch of cardboard. Fleet struggled out of the hot, cramped box and sat shakily beside it. Bertha and Rook looked all over him for damage and found none, to their great relief.

Fleet was rather shaken from the long time he'd spent frightened in Quickbuck's pocket and the shoe box. 'I thought I'd never see you again,' he admitted to them both. 'How could you have known I was at the railway station?'

Rook told him about the crystal ball.

'What about our eggs, Bertha?' Fleet asked. 'I suppose they'll be cold and no good now.'

Bertha looked at him uncertainly. 'I don't know,' she answered, 'I don't know if they'll be all right or not.'

There was nothing she could add. She was thinking about the blood round Tired Melvin's feathered feet. His sharp black talons beside the eggs, or chicks, whichever they were by this time.

Anyway there were more immediate problems. Although Fleet was freed from the parcel and they were together, the awful fact remained that they were trapped in a train which was speeding closer and closer to London. What about when they arrived there? What about the moment when the train stopped and somebody opened the great crashing wagon door? What would they do then? How could they get home? Bertha and Rook didn't know. They turned to Fleet.

'You *must* stay by me,' he said. 'I'm a homing pigeon and I shall be able to feel the way to go.'

'But how will you *see*, Fleet?' asked Rook anxiously. 'It's so dark and none of us have ever been to London before.'

'I have,' replied Fleet, 'and it may not matter about the light, I mightn't need it, I fly by the pull of the earth and by ways homing pigeons have known for hundreds of years. If only we had some food. It's bad for us racing pigeons to fly weak with hunger, it affects our judgement of distance and direction.'

'There's a bit of chicken meal spilt on the floor over here,' offered Soothsayer Rook from a gloomy corner. 'You have it, Fleet, you're leading us.'

'Oh, no,' Fleet answered, 'we'll share it. We'll all need our strength. This railway train passes over the ground faster than you can guess. It will be a long hard journey if we are ever to see our homes again.'

A hint of coldness ran through Rook's feathers. He was an old Rook and not very fit. He thought of his home in the dead elms. There were no leaves any more and the wood had a dry cracked feel about it he didn't care for, but it was home. The branch he lived on was worn smooth and shiny from his feet. He knew the creaking of the wood there, the way the wind sang. The thought of never seeing it again filled Rook with despair. He had never tried to fly long distances; pigeons were different, of course. He pecked at the dusty meal on the floor, but had no appetite.

Bertha watched him from her perch beside Fleet on the mailbag. She thought about the day he'd told her fortune and she hadn't listened. He had seen it all, the long journey, Paddington, the word that began with P. What a true friend Rook was, swooping down from the station roof into the wagon, and facing Harry Crackitt in the door. Rook could have gone to his safe home and left Bertha to cope as best she could, but he hadn't.

And so they waited. Close together on the mailbag they faced the door, feeling for the slowing of the train and frightened, all of them. Only Fleet's head was a little higher than the others, his eye a little brighter. He was a Red-Checkered Racing Homer, and he had to get them home. It was up to him.

21

Back home in Harris House, Quickbuck undid the nine locks on the drinks cupboard to reveal the bottle of whisky and tin of peanuts they saved for Christmas and Quickbuck's birthday.

'I think, my son,' said Quickbuck to his brother, 'I think my amazing resourcefulness in procuring us twenty pounds for a spot of pigeon catching calls for a little celebration.' He took down two cups from the shelf. 'What did you say you were going to spend your two pounds on?' The stunned look came back to Andy's face and his white eyebrows travelled up and down in alarm.

They drank the whisky and watched the fire crackle and smack in the grate. Then they drank a little more whisky and Andy started to eat peanuts from the tin. When the whisky bottle was empty, Quickbuck got up from his chair closely followed by a spring and slapped Andy a sickening blow on the back. The tin in Andy's hand erupted and peanuts shot all ways. 'The Rod and Maggot, my son!' announced Quickbuck.

Together they stumbled across the fields the back way to the pub. The illuminated plump maggot on the inn sign beckoned them on. Andy began to sing a little touching ballad as they clambered over the fence into the yard. Quickbuck lengthened his stride past the littered beer crates and steel barrels. Looking back, he seized Andy's arm to hurry him along. They stepped out into space and two horrified shouts rang out as Andy and Quickbuck Harris plunged downwards into the mud at the bottom of Sheik Wish Ida Bought One's hole. A terrible silence seeped up from the depths. Then Andy's voice, wailing and plaintive, cried, 'You're sitting on my spur!'

And Quickbuck Harris, face crazed with pain, replied through gritted teeth, 'I know.'

22

Now Paddington Station in London is an enormous place full of noise and bustle and, above all, people. There are trains on either side as far as you can see, funny sharp-nosed trains that travel like the wind and cosy flat-faced trains that go more slowly. Swerving round the platforms are taxis and long rows of luggage-filled trucks and over all hangs a great clock so you can see how many minutes you missed the train by.

People run and weave everywhere, people crying, kissing, hitting each other and drinking too much. People with boxes and bags, people carrying suitcases in their arms because the lock broke. People hollering and shouting 'Mind your backs!' as if your fronts didn't matter. And into this frantic neon lit scene drew the 6.30 p.m. from Wanford Road Station.

23

The train came to a halt. All round Bertha, Fleet and Sooth-sayer Rook were strange noises, muffled shouting, whistles and footsteps running back and forth. Their wagon rocked violently as the door of the next one was slammed back. They heard the thud of mailbags being flung out on the platform. They waited stiff, their hearts pounding. Fleet was in the centre. Heavy footsteps halted outside their door. The lock rattled sharply as it was unfastened.

'Stay with *me*,' Fleet told them urgently. 'Follow me wherever I go.'

The others nodded, poised. The door crashed back. Light blazed into the wagon dazzling them all. Three men stood in the door, wearing hats and uniforms.

'Good grief!' exclaimed one, pointing.

'Now!' said Fleet.

The three birds flew for the door together. The men, startled, ducked aside shouting as Rook's big black wings clapped noisily. Then they were out and up towards the ceiling of the station, up in the great steel girders and iron, flying blindly in the noise and smoke and terrifying bright light. Down on the ground the three men continued to shout and point. 'Blow me if it isn't a blooming old rook! Get my air gun!' one of the men shouted excitedly.

Fleet seemed to be barging round in circles. 'It's like a great big shed!' cried Rook in despair. 'We can't get *out*!'

'Yes, we can!' Fleet cried back. 'One end is open for the trains to come in! There, look! Fly for the end!'

Behind Fleet they dodged through the great iron framework supporting the roof, making for the dark gap at the end that was sky and freedom. A train appeared, edging in, hissing, with great blazing headlamps which would have frightened Rook and Bertha back into the main station but Fleet flew on towards it, passing above it with the others following him closely, trusting and hoping.

Then they were out, in the clear sky. The wet streets below them were stained with great bands of light from shops. Traffic was roaring in all directions. Fleet flew up and up into the open sky and then flew level, sweeping in a wide circle, again and again, listening for the call of home, waiting.

'This way!' he called joyfully. 'This way . . . to the west!' and he veered out on a straight path. Bertha and Rook flew

behind, watching as his pale body settled into even, effortless flight against the black sky. It had stopped raining. Rook flew hard, puffing quietly. His feet as always were clasping the marble. It was his livelihood but, more than that, it was a comfort and a friend. He had not looked into it. For once, he didn't want to see.

But the journey had begun.

24

Tired Melvin had the cramp. He thanked his lucky stars that none of the other owls could see him now, sitting on two eggs in a pigeons' nest. What would they *say* to him? Melvin went cold at the thought. He couldn't imagine why he had agreed to do it. Bertha and Rook had taken advantage of his half-asleep state, he fumed to himself up in the corner. And the eggs wouldn't keep still! They kept shifting around under him, bending his fine chest feathers back the wrong way and irritating him. And where could they *be*, these pigeons? They were the Day Shift, they did their living in the sunshine and light so what were they doing now, out in the dark? How much longer was he supposed to wait?

Besides, he was growing hungry. This was the time he went out, at night when he was wide awake, alert and cunning.

This was the time he drifted silently along the hedgerows like a shadow, huge eyes wide and watching. He watched all the time, looking for a movement, a rustle, a small noise not made by the wind or by a twig falling, but by a Little Living Thing. Then he would hover to make sure, but the little victim wouldn't ever see him up there, scanning each blade of grass. All there would be was the sudden blocking out of light from above and the pain of great sharp claws as the owl dropped down to take it. The little living thing would squeak a bit and that was all. The owl would swoop away into the cold rushing air and eat his fill.

Melvin grew hungrier and crosser by the minute. All his instincts urged him to leave the Barn, the cramped ridiculous nest.

Suddenly something sharp stuck into the Owl's chest. Jumping nervously, he sprang up, looking down alarmed at the eggs. He stared, incredulous. A beak was showing through the shell of one egg! It had cracked! And there inside, wriggling, was a Little Living Thing. . . .

25

It had started to rain again. Poor Rook was lagging far behind. Still clinging loyally to the marble he flew in a jerky mechanical fashion, low in the sky. It seemed they had flown all night long, over endless black woodlands and bright towns. Rook no longer noticed the features of the land below. There was terrible pain in his wings and in his bones. Rook's eyes were half closed and he flew blindly. His home seemed a million miles away and he felt old, dreadfully old and useless. The pigeons were so swift, but then they were spurred on by anxiety about their babies. Rook blundered on clumsily in the darkness and the rain.

Fleet was keeping a worried, careful eye on him. To Bertha flying alongside he said quietly, 'We will have to rest. Rook is in a very bad way.'

He called back, 'Rook! we're going to rest, this fir tree up ahead, follow us!'

It was a big fir tree, the kind that stood in Wanford Market at Christmas all covered in lights. Bertha and Fleet helped Rook to wedge himself between the tree trunk and a big branch. They could see he was almost finished. Fleet leant close to his ear and said, 'It isn't far now, Rook; I can't be sure but I feel we are almost home.'

Rook shook his head. 'You'll have to leave me behind,' he said. 'I'm sorry, Fleet. I hoped I would turn out to be a long-distance rook but I haven't.' He puffed his feathers up

and closed his eyes, his head leaning sideways on the trunk of
the Christmas tree.

'No!' chorused Bertha and Fleet together, 'we won't do that,
leave you propped up here after you've helped us so much.
You *must* fly a little further, Rook, just a few more fields.'

'But what about your eggs?' asked Rook. 'I'm slowing you
both down.'

'We don't care!' insisted the pigeons. 'We won't go home
without you.'

'Try to fly on, Rook,' Fleet said. 'I'll take your crystal ball
for a while.'

So they flew down from the Christmas tree and journeyed
on for twenty minutes more. The pigeons flew with heavy
hearts, one eye fearfully on Rook.

Fleet was searching desperately for landmarks.

Suddenly his sharp eye caught the shape of one solitary rooftop in the distance, silhouetted black against the moonlight. He looked at it, looked to the east and west to make certain, then cried out loud, 'Rook! It's the Fruit Pie Factory!'

Rook opened one eye disbelievingly and saw the familiar shape. 'It's the Fruit Pie Factory,' he said reassuringly to himself. A great tear appeared, ran down his white beak and

mingled with the rain. New strength flowed into his aching wings. There, on the horizon, were the dead elms; Rook was nearly home!

They dropped down over the familiar factory and turned to cross the last few fields to the Barn. Bertha was desperately afraid for the babies. She had been away for so *long*. 'I couldn't help it, babies,' she thought. 'I had to go after Fleet. I didn't want to leave you but I had no choice.'

Now they could make out the shape of the Barn. It had never looked so welcoming. With their feet outstretched for landing, marble and all, they streamed in through the great barn door clapping their tired wings. Bertha made straight for the Upper Right-Hand Corner.

Tired Melvin was standing to one side of the nest, staring in. He jumped violently as Bertha arrived beside him. There in the nest, in a disgusting state of not-having-been-cleaned-up-yet, were two beautiful white chicks, stuck all over with pieces of shell and peering anxiously this way and that. The babies were safe! Not only that, they were by far the most beautiful babies Bertha had ever seen!

'Oh, Melvin,' said Bertha, 'whatever can we say to you?'

'Well!' exploded the Owl. 'Well! You might *start* by saying *sorry*! Do you know how *long* I've sat here? I'm half mad with hunger! Oh, no,' he declared, shaking his head fussily, 'I have no wish to Detract from your Natural Joy, of course, but I do feel that Incompatibility has Attained Untenable Proportions.'

Bertha blinked. 'What does that mean, Melvin?' she asked in a small voice.

'It means I shall move into the cowshed round the back,' stated the Owl firmly. 'Good day!'

Owl swooped low out of the Barn, white and mothy, to begin his overdue hunting expedition.

'Thank you very much, Melvin,' the pigeons chorused after him. Fleet and Bertha set about separating the chicks from the sticky eggshell.

'I say,' croaked down Soothsayer Rook who, reunited with the crystal ball, was squinting into it high up in the rafters of the Barn. 'The crystal ball is clearin'! It shows a great family of brown and white and grey pigeons sitting on the roof of a barn. As far as I can see,' he announced, 'they all live happily ever after.'

He rolled the marble safely up into the corner. 'And,' he added, settling down to sleep, 'we Long-Distance Rooks are Never Wrong.'